a new year's toy

EVA MARKS

Copyright © 2022 by Eva Marks

All rights reserved.

No part of this publication may be reproduced, distributed, or transmitted in any form or by any means, including photocopying, recording, or other electronic or mechanical methods, without the prior written permission of the publisher, except as permitted by U.S. copyright law. For permission requests, contact authorevamarks@gmail.com

The story, all names, characters, and incidents portrayed in this production are fictitious. No identification with actual persons (living or deceased), places, buildings, and products is intended or should be inferred.

Book Cover by Eva Marks

A Note from the Author

A New Year's Toy is a steamy novella, containing explicit and graphic scenes and kinks intended for mature audiences only.

Trigger Warnings
Contains BDSM, sadist-masochist relationship, Daddy kink, bondage, breath play, lots of toys, some degradation.

About the Book

Paris, here we come.
I'm living my dream life. With a hot, caring boyfriend and a self-owned adult toy shop, I'm the happiest I've ever been.

But I can't rest. Now that I have my shop, I want to evolve, to add new items you can't find in the US. Exclusive additions to my shop that are only available in Paris, the city of love.

This New Year's Eve, Alistair, will join me on this business trip.

My sweet sadist, my Daddy. My soulmate. My teacher of all things naughty. Whether I'm wearing my business suit...

Or not.

CHAPTER ONE
Nora

Tears stream down like rivers along the length of my cheeks.

Two or three catch at the strands of my messy brown hair, dampening it.

Another two land on the wall-to-wall carpet. Two blotches that darken the dense, cream fibers.

Though they aren't the only things to drop to the floor.

The cane that served to land blows on my behind produces a soft thud when it meets with the plush fabric. The remote control for the butt plug is next in line.

"Good girl."

Alistair's lips are at my shoulder, his short stubble at my neck. His chiseled arm envelopes my belly from underneath, supporting my body weight since my shaky arms nearly lose the battle of holding me on the coffee table.

"Hold still, sweetheart." He removes the silicone toy from my butt in one long, careful motion.

My boyfriend of five months has taken our sex toy classes to a whole new level today.

His cock possessed my cunt, the new toys I brought owned the rest of me; the vibrating butt plug my behind, the cane condemning my ass and thighs to one brutal yet calculated blow one after the other.

And while I feel my skin swelling from the thrashing, a swift thought runs through my head. I did well to order the new cane with the option to add a rubber cover on it to smooth out the blows.

The clients of my shop, We Love You, are going to love it.

After months of working in a high-end, yet completely unethical sex shop, my business plan gained me a grant to open up the store as I envisioned it to be.

An ethical place. Somewhere I don't have to call some of the customers in secret, offering them free of charge non-life-threatening products instead of those Roger, my former manager, had up for sale.

Even though it's how I met Alistair, I still hate the place. I remember vividly how out of the entire merchandise his online order—for the woman he stopped seeing shortly before I called him—he hadn't chosen one single decent product.

He couldn't have known, of course. They were marketed as the top of the line. This was true for some toys in our store. Some. Not these.

But behind my mask of continuous detest of the place, I can't forget that was the day I met him. How he got curious about me, how he offered to teach me about the toys I'd never played with, myself.

Sigh.

He supported me from the start, supported me when I opened the shop thanks to a grant I received, and supports me now as I operate it. Including, but not limited to, experimenting with the toys before we offer them to my clients.

It warms my heart; it truly does. This forty-two-year-old billionaire, owner, and CEO of the largest solar energy provider in the US and many other businesses is always there for me.

The word *no* doesn't leave his mouth. Whenever I ask him to try a new product, he's there to play with me.

He has a million things to do. He works long hours, sometimes having late-night video calls with suppliers from overseas.

Still, he carves the time. Doesn't keep me waiting.

His universe revolves solely around me.

His Nolita. His sweetheart.

His good little student.

He kisses my cheek after the butt plug is gone. "Such a good girl to take a beating like that."

A beating and an earth-shattering orgasm. I still can't decide which was harder to endure.

"Thank you, Daddy." I manage between sobs that his care helps simmer out.

The physical pain drains away as Alistair places me on a soft cushion. The sofa he has me on offers a view of the lake his home in Medina, Seattle overlooks. It's soothing. It's peaceful. It's becoming my home.

Alistair swaddles me in a thermal throw blanket. Warming flames lick at the stone walls of Alistair's fireplace, and yet it's not enough to fight the cold December in Seattle.

Especially in my naked state, emotionally and physically.

With my body covered, Alistair unfolds himself to his six feet two inches. He throws on his gray sweatpants and matching Henley shirt. He rakes his fingers through his short, straight dark-blond hair in an attempt to smooth it, then he sits at my side.

His thigh brushes mine, his thumbs wipe the salty water off my cheeks and jaw, clearing a wayward lock off my face.

"Here." He beckons me to take the thermos of tea we set near us before we started this evening. "Drink this."

I prefer Alistair's warmth over tea, but I take it without arguing. He's a firm believer in aftercare and grounding me, and I trust him to always have my best intentions in mind.

While I drink in small sips, he dabs a plush, white cloth in a bowl of lukewarm water. I study him behind the rim of the thermos.

He lifts the bottom of the blanket, gently parting my legs to allow him access. There's an immense tenderness to how he pats the insides of my thighs. He treats my bum with equal gentle care, lifting me to pat it lovingly.

"We'll have to apply ointment on you." He levels me with a meaningful stare once he's done. "But I'd like to talk first for a few minutes. I'm concerned."

I take another drink of my tea. Chamomile has such a soothing quality.

So does honesty.

Skipping on dancing around the subject, I ask, "About the tears?"

A wide range of emotions tend to flare in Alistair's smirk—filthy thoughts, conspiring scenes, and sometimes, like today, it's a smirk that says *I see you* and *thank you for not hiding it from me*.

"You said yourself you needed this session today, not to just try out the new toys." He brushes the corner of my eye, Swiping away the residue of a tear.

Yes, Alistair and I test and enjoy my products and are rough about it.

But it didn't start this way for him.

He's aware of the therapeutic benefits of sadomasochism, of why I asked for it as a way to work out my stress, because he's been using it for the longest time to get over his own issues.

Years ago, Alistair's younger sister went out for a fun day of diving into the sea from cliffs with friends and his mom asked him to look after her. Since Connie had done it plenty in the past, he trusted her to be fine. He stayed at home to work on his developing business.

Connie never returned from that trip. It wasn't Alistair's fault. He couldn't have done anything even if he'd been there. In his heart, none of that mattered.

He hated himself, hated Mother Nature for stealing his sister from him. His loathing burned bright in a fire he kept trying to put out ever since through sadism.

It's how he handled his grief and the loss of control that day brought him for over twenty years. Being the bearer of pain and deliverer of pleasure all at once gave him a sense of power, chasing off the nightmares. If only for a while.

He's been doing better, our love and talks definitely help. But he remembers how it helped him. He engulfs me with his kind of cruel love always, letting me know he's not like my ex from high school who dumped me shortly after we started having sex.

And he's that more conscious of it when I tell him in advance that I need to relieve my own stress.

"But it appears I miscalculated the severity of it." His brown eyes lighten, soften around the edges. "Is there anything other than the shop stressing you out?"

"No…"

Before I get to finish my reply, Alistair places the teas aside. He's careful of my sore body, hoists me off the sofa, spreads his legs, and positions my wounded behind between them.

His lips press to the top of my head. I melt into his chest. The physical pain is forgotten, the cane a distant memory. I lean into Alistair, finding comfort in his broad, hard chest, clinging to his shirt.

"You know you can tell me anything," he cajoles.

He refers to himself as *me* instead of *Daddy*, but there's no doubt in mind that he means to say it. I sure as shit feel it. Alistair prioritizes me, provides advice if I ask for it, and on rare occasions chooses my outfits.

He does it affectionately, doesn't overstep any lines. Isn't overbearing, isn't suffocating. Alistair is Daddy simply because he's the epitome of love.

"The shop is doing well. Really well."

"I see that." He wraps the blanket around me so other than my head, not an inch of my body is exposed. "I see you."

I shift in his lap, tilting my head up. "Some days, I want to do everything. Then I do it, more marketing, reorganizing the shelves like I saw on YouTube, reaching out to new suppliers. It keeps me going, but sometimes it's a lot. I should feel grateful for every minute of it. Why is that?"

"You love that shop."

"I do."

His arm around my shoulders tightens, the other hand slides beneath the blanket, running up and down my thighs.

His shaft hardens, poking the side of my body. My core is wet again. Yet, neither of us comments on it. Our attraction is undeniable, but so is our emotional connection.

"You can love something and still admit pouring yourself into it takes a toll on you," he says, his voice smooth, patient, and understanding. "We can postpone the trip to Paris, celebrate New Year's Eve at home. Taking a step back could do you good."

"No. I'm looking forward to it." My lips press to his jaw, ever grateful for his presence in my life. "In case I haven't said it enough, thank you for going along with my crazy idea."

"Nola." My name is a demand to return his gaze. "I'm proud of you. So damn proud of you. Joining you on your business trip to Paris, to be there when you sign an exclusive contract you worked hard to get, it's my absolute pleasure. My honor. I'm the grateful one, sweetheart."

The beating organ in my chest pulses to an erratic rhythm. My love for Alistair, for the protector he is. For the genuine flavor of his words that never fails to translate into his actions.

I'm hot for him all over again. Want to get lost in him for days.

A luxury neither of us has... At the moment.

In less than a couple of hours, we'll have an abundance of time on his private jet.

Alone.

He and I and no one else, tapping into one special game we've studied over the past two months with a splash of a couple of toys of my own.

CHAPTER TWO
Alistair

"Unless the plane is about to crash," I say to Rory, my flight attendant, "do not knock on this door. For anything."

"What about lunch for you and Ms. Vickers, Mr. Cromwell?"

I don't bother correcting her to address me on a first-name basis.

There are more important matters than tending to unnecessary formalities.

My girlfriend.

My eyes skate to Nola. She's stunning in the skin-tight gray dress and cream-colored flats I left for her next to the bed we share.

She offers me a sly smile. I smirk in return.

She loves me.

It's a concept that continues to baffle me. Five months later, to love and to be loved remains a mystery I accept step by step.

Nola is there constantly. Regardless of my past fuckups, our rocky start.

She deems me worthy of giving me her heart every day anew.

I'm humbled to be the receiver of such a precious gift, and the best I can do is give her mine in return.

Hopefully, by the end of this trip, for life.

"We'll find you," I address Rory, though my thoughts are centered exclusively on Nola.

"All right, sir."

Rory stalks toward the front of the plane, passing the mahogany tables, leather couches, disappearing behind a heavy, gray curtain separating the flight attendants' area from ours.

I turn to look at Nola. She's left my side, already by the door to the bedroom, kicking her shoes off. She has her back to me, carrying the small duffle she brought.

Nola isn't shy about showing me her new toys. Usually. I'm confident she carries some in her bag, and my mouth salivates at what's inside.

At what I'm going to do to her during the ten hours we have on our flight.

"Been sneaking surprises onto the plane?" A soft click of the lock shuts the world and the rest of the crew outside.

"Since we have some time to burn on the flight…" My five-foot-seven temptress twists to me, biting the side of her lip.

Flirting.

I'm hard, my need for her pressing inside my blue jeans. The game is on.

I flick my wrist to the bag she's holding. "Let me see what's inside."

"I've been meaning to ask for your opinion." She passes it on to me. "And play."

It's heavier than I would've expected and now I'm not just humbled to have her share her work with me. I'm intrigued.

"New products?" I tilt my head, schooling my expression.

As proud as I am of her, as much as a smile begs to crack through my lips, I bottle up these feelings. There's no room for them moments before I inflict a generous amount of pain on her, to make it appear like I'm any less in control.

"Yes." Her fingers toy with the sleeve of her shirt, tugging it lower on her arm.

The thin, black strap of her bra appears. The top of the lace cup too.

"My busy little bee."

Pretending not to notice her exposed skin, I walk past her, sitting on the edge of the bed. I'm ravenous in my want to pin her to the floor facedown, but how fucking boring would that be?

"I thought you said you were overwhelmed."

"It's been humming around in my head since Christmas." She swivels in place on her bare feet to face me. "A ton of people were asking to package a few items as a gift, and it got me thinking about this."

I pat the bag in my lap for her to join me, which she does. On her knees. Some days I feed her in this position, others I wrap my hand around her throat and listen to her strangled breaths, how she gives them to me.

Nola's long brown locks drape to the front of her body, though they do little to hide the outline of her nipples through her dress. I want to slap them. Want to reproach her for acting without my permission for the sake of hearing her gasp at the sting of my palm.

But I sense that whatever's inside that bag holds much more potential than a banal smack.

The zipper slides to the left. Three packages lie before me—a large one in red, a medium one in cyan, the smallest one in purple. I lift the purple one, unwrapping it and opening the brown lid of the box. It contains handcuffs, a blindfold, a suction vibrator, anal beads, and a cock ring.

"Gift boxes." I place everything back. Another surge of delight courses through me. Most new businesses aim to survive. My Nola, she shoots for the peak of the mountain. "For Christmas, birthdays, Valentine's."

"Yes." She nods enthusiastically.

"Smart girl."

"Thank you, Daddy." Her voice is breathless, her heightened arousal practically coating the room. "Open the largest one. It's for you."

Her request means consulting time is over. The rest of the bag goes to the floor after I take out the red package, tear the wrapper and open it. A sadistic smirk tugs at my lips.

Between, under, and all around the five toys inside the box, there are so many black bondage ribbons. We've been experimenting for a couple of months on more elaborate knots with Paul, our private instructor, so I don't damage her in the process.

Time to put his lessons to the test. Sans clothes.

I free my hands, lowering to kneel beside Nola. The minidress that's been taunting me on the ride over goes first. I start at the hem, sliding the elastic fabric over her head and throwing it to the side.

"This isn't going to be nice." I snap the hatch of her bra, discarding it somewhere in the background.

"We never do nice."

"Goddamn right."

With a hand around her lower back, I pull her to me. The movement is harsh, a whip forcing her to arch her back. Her nipples are in my face, and I bite and torture the left while twisting and kneading her right breast between punishing fingers.

"You wet for me?" I murmur to her reddening flesh.

"Yes," she gasps, completely at my mercy.

"You want me to use the items in here? On you?"

"Yes." Her legs tremble as her nipples harden under my ministrations. "I want you, all the time."

My head snaps up. "You're gonna wish you didn't say that."

Instead of being horrified, Nola's eyes go half-mast. All pleasure, without the pain the both of us cherish. I'll have to rectify that.

"On the bed." I get up, jerking my head toward the made sheets. "Quick."

Nola scrambles to her feet, walking fast to come lie on her back. She spreads her knees for me, showing me her slickness through the thin lace of her panties.

"Greedy little girl." I pinch my stubbled chin, pretending to contemplate what to do with her next.

It's a pretense. I know exactly what.

With one knee on the mattress, I go about removing the remaining fabric separating Nola's cunt from me.

"Don't move." I glare down at her. She nods, mouthing the word yes.

Retrieving the small pair of scissors from the gift box, I place the dull part of the inner blade on her thigh. Nola squirms at the touch of the cold metal on her skin.

"I said,"—I press her thigh forcefully to the bed, opening her up more—"don't. Move."

"Okay." Her teeth sink into her bottom lip.

I thrive on her skin breaking, her tears leaking, the saliva dripping down her chin when she gags on my cock. Not fear that I'll do something we haven't discussed with the potential to harm her.

"Nola." My fingers alternate between squeezing the flesh of her thigh and caressing it.

"Yeah?" The mixture of pain and fear has her somewhat floaty.

I quit stroking her. I grab her, hard.

"Nola."

"Yes?" Her eyes are a bit more lucid, her throat clears.

"What's your safeword? What do you tell me when it gets too much?"

She blinks once, focusing on me. Her breasts still rise and fall with heavy breathing, but she manages to say it anyway, "Red."

"That's my girl."

My fingers pinch her tight little mound over her underwear. Nola growls in pain, then thrusts her hips up to my gently massaging fingers.

"I'll never, ever go to an extreme such as cutting you without asking your permission. I'm just going to…" The blades of the scissors close in on her waistband, a shark preparing to snap its jaws on its prey. "Cut these off."

In an instant, the fabric falls to either side of her. I leave the scissors closed for the ribbons and peel off Nola's underwear.

"I'm sorry," she says once I'm done.

"Don't." I flip Nola on her stomach, back to our scene to where it was before the sight of the scissors scared my poor woman. My hands run over the oily skin and red welts. "This one's all on me. I'm sorry, sweetheart."

"That's okay." She fixes her head so she's gazing at me through her mass of hair. "Please don't stop, I'm good."

"Baby."

Assessing the length of the ribbon I need, I cut it and hover over Nola's naked body. I'm hard again, looking at her dripping pussy, her fine round ass. Knowing they're mine to do with as I please.

"Stopping is the last thing that's on my mind."

CHAPTER THREE
Nola

"Oh," is the one literate word I'm capable of uttering.

His large, toned frame casts the shadow I've loved since that moment five months ago in his private room in the back of his bar. When we were complete strangers, where he taught me the joy of sex and stripped the hesitation attached to it.

His ominous looming plays as the prelude to his measured brutality, the first act of the play we're both leads in.

"My dirty girl."

He slips the ribbon between my back and joint hands. The fabric slides smoothly across my skin. It's silky.

Soft.

A stark contrast to the tie Alistair bounds my wrists with.

"You didn't have other people in mind when you curated the red box, didn't you?"

I bite the inside of my cheek to suffocate my smirk. Of course, I didn't.

How could I? This man plagues my thoughts, hijacks my days and nights alike.

And sure, other people might and probably will entertain themselves using a paddle that's one side leather, the other fur. They'll more than likely appreciate the particular rabbit vibrator I included.

Judging by my clients' feedback on the products, they'll love those two, the ribbon, and the rest of the added toys compiling this box. Really love them.

But their meaning won't be as sacred to them as it is to us. Both the paddle and vibrator were two of the toys Alistair used on me in our early days together, and he's right to guess it's why they're in there.

"No, I didn't."

He digs into my skin with his fingers, flipping me on my back. My lungs heave out a surprised breath, while the rest of my body is epically ready for him. Tingles break out on my skin, my breasts are heavy as lust takes over my very existence.

A current of desire thrums in my pussy, an immediate response to Alistair's gauging stare, to the sex dripping from his eyes.

"I don't think about anyone but you, Daddy."

"Such a good girl. And sneaky." His eyes darken. "I would've used this little piece of nostalgia to rain pain and pleasure on you. Still would, though they won't be the stars of the show. Something else piqued my interest."

He doesn't tell me which one. Doesn't glance in its direction.

What he does is parts my legs, forcing my knees to the sides of my breasts. He lies on top of me, pressing his cock to my pussy. It's hard in his jeans, and I'm pulsating, needing it bare, dying for it to slide and slap on my skin.

To have Alistair bury this thick piece of flesh into me.

"Don't move." His fingers curl around my neck, his thumb drawing circles on my pulsing vein. "I feel your orgasm building, Nola, you know that? I can sense it, can see it in your eyes."

"Yes."

The anticipation he's generated runs ever strong through me.

I'm pretty sure I'll combust at the slightest flick of his tongue.

Pretty sure he'll withhold it from me for long, long minutes, too.

Yet, I still ask, "I want to. Can I?"

Alistair delivers another surprise by slithering down the path of my body, parting my lips, and growling, "Yes."

His hot breath on my clit sends my eyes rolling to the back of my head, the lap of his tongue yanking out a desperate cry from the depths of my lungs.

My legs spread and my hands are tied. I'm at Alistair's mercy, knowing what's to come.

It never does. The anticipation of cruelty is unmatched by reality. Alistair has three fingers pumping into me gently. He doesn't bite my mound, he sucks on it, kissing it.

I would've been suspicious, except I lack any sort of mental capacity for it. I'm subjected to the pleasure Alistair bestows on me and nothing else, allowing him to carry me gracefully to my promised orgasm.

In what seems like mere seconds, I call out his name, my ass gyrating to meet more of his fingers and tongue. I'm in a state of bliss.

"Beautiful, voluntary orgasm." He licks my juices off his glistening lips.

Voluntary?

He reads the question bursting through my sated expression. "The next few won't be. Not until I come in your mouth."

My head flops back with a sigh. It doesn't sound so bad. We've done sixty-nine before, or he'd fuck me for hours then take it out last minute to have his cum drip down my tongue.

Alistair, who controls his orgasms just like he controls me, takes his sweet time with it, too. I've grown accustomed to the ache entailed in three or four orgasms coaxed out of me in a night.

I can take it.

I'm usually able to but I discover quickly today, I cannot.

Alistair reaches the cardboard box, extracting the wand vibrator out of it.

"Oh," I let out the helpless word again.

He holds the toy that doesn't simply force orgasms, it coerces them to rise over and over again. There will be many, many more than three orgasms today. Or maybe there won't be many, but they'll be ones Alistair will undoubtedly demand me to prolong.

The coming torture scares and elates me. I take on both feelings, hold on to them, and wait.

"*Oh* is the correct response to the game you and I are about to play."

Alistair removes the wand from its plastic box, using the wipes I added to clean it. He continues to fish out the paddle, placing them both next to the remaining ribbon.

His belt, dark blue sweater, and the navy long-sleeved T-shirt he has beneath it come off. I'm mesmerized anew at the defined planes of his stomach, the smattering of the hair covering it, leading below his jeans. He discards those as well, along with his boxer briefs.

What a glorious, proud, and erect man he is.

A predatory man.

"Legs together."

The request is a command, one he gives me no time to fulfill. He yanks both my feet to the edge of the bed, tying me at the ankles.

Snap, the scissors go.

I'm slowly being transformed into Alistair's gift, the way he ties the bow so neatly.

I want it. I want to be his however he takes me. Whether he's sweet or torturous or both, I want it all.

With one hand he lifts my feet in the air, positioning them on his left shoulder. The other, he wraps around his length. I'm unable to watch the act since my legs hide the view from me, but by the angle of his right arm, the straining of his bicep, I know exactly what he's doing.

He observes me, a lion gauging a lamb. "Before anything, sweetheart, I'm gonna fuck your pussy. Just for a little."

The blunt crown of his dick parts my folds. At this angle, given how closed my legs are, I'm tight, blocking his entrance. Alistair probes harder, the force of nature he is, and grunts when he fills me up to the hilt.

"Yes." He pummels into me. "Take it, take it all."

Despite the tearing feeling of my insides, the strain of the binds on my hands and feet, I do. I'm wet, and yet it doesn't help the sting of his brutal invasion. My face twitches until I start accommodating his size in this position, one ravenous stroke after the other.

He curses under his breath when he pulls out. His hair is mussed, eyes devouring me whole.

"Greedy girl with a greedy cunt," are his final words before he throws my legs to the side.

They hit the bed, the plush mattress absorbing my fall. I barely straighten myself when Alistair returns from the other side of the bed, carrying the wand like a beacon.

"I don't need to explain to you what this is." He lays it between my thighs, the head of it resting on my rapidly awakening clit. "I'll turn it on, though you're not to come of your own volition. Only I have the power to allow you to come."

I nod, eager for him to start. I'd been afraid of sex before, of the emotional damage giving this part of me to someone might bring. Since I met Alistair, however, I don't just run—I sprint toward it.

His skillful hands tie two extra bows around my legs. One at the bottom of the wand, one in the middle of it, locking the toy to my body so I can't shake it off.

"That'll work." He admires his work and turns the switch on.

My hips jerk in the air, the impulse to get rid of the violent pulse of arousal choking me. I'm still turned on by having Alistair's cock in me from how he fucked me a moment earlier, from having Alistair shatter me with his hungry, unfathomable look.

From watching my boyfriend watch me back, fisting his hard shaft in slow, languid strokes.

This wand, this fucking orgasm-commanding wand, intensifies these sensations not by a million—but by infinity.

"Alistair," I croak out his name.

Thrones of desire eclipse my existence. Only Alistair remains my light, the dominator of my world. He who reigns my kingdom.

The owner and Daddy who can swipe the pain away.

Which is the opposite of what my sadist intends to do.

"Hush, now." His palm rests on my thigh, forcing me down to the bed.

"I'm about to…"

"Hold on."

"I need…"

The words are strained, each intake of breath more painful than the previous one. The throbbing in my clit, the rising orgasm threaten to swallow me inside out.

"What you need is to be good."
"No," I whimper, sucking in my lips.
"Yes."

Eventually, the primal, uncontainable desire prevails between the both of us. The climax that slashes me in half starts where the wand keeps vibrating, up my navel, my sternum, my throat. Groaning, grunting, and moaning, I thrash my head to where Alistair is supposed to be, looking for him.

I find him, his hand holding my arms and leg, flipping me to my side.

CHAPTER FOUR
Nora

Smack.

He starts with the leather side of the paddle. This isn't his usual cruel strike, given the state my ass is in, but fuck, does it hurt.

"You're warmed up now," he clarifies why he didn't use the fur side to begin with. Why he doesn't hit me with it the second time the paddle flags my flesh. "And you've disobeyed me. This guarantees you won't do it again today."

My swollen center hasn't had a moment to recuperate. Alistair left the wand on, buzzing in the air between us. A whisper in the wind saying *come, come, come.*

Alistair angles the paddle so it's perpendicular to my body. He dips the edge to the stripe where my butt cheeks meet, sliding it up and down. It chafes and arouses me in a magical, torturous combination, a blast of cold and hot water jets all at once.

Insanely confusing, remarkably awakening.

"No." He yanks it up when my ass clenches around it, the moment my body nearly goes against Alistair's orders and readies itself for another torment of an orgasm.

Five smacks follow. For a slim, lucid second, I wonder if the room is soundproofed or if the flight crew can hear us. On Alistair's sixth strike, I decide I don't care.

Alistair isn't bothered by it, either.

He shifts me around on my back, straddling my locked legs.

"You think you learned?" He trails the hot paddle to my breast, slapping it tenderly with the fur side. "Can I trust you to be well-behaved when I'm busy fucking your mouth?"

"Yes," I grunt, squeezing my legs tight, commanding my focus off the wand and on the man who owns my heart, body, and soul.

"Yes, what?" Alistair tosses the paddle, advancing up on my body. His cock grazes my skin. It's slick with my arousal, my sweat, and soon with my spit.

"Yes, Daddy."

"Correct." He caresses my face, kissing my forehead in one of his unnatural, kind gestures before he looks deep into my eyes. "I'm checking in. How are your wrists? Your arms?"

His love doesn't break the scene for me; it enhances it. His caring side doesn't take away his sadistic side, simply makes him that much more my king.

"I'm okay," I blurt out, then swallow down another orgasm.

He smirks, reverting to the punishing man he is during scenes.

Alistair's lips are in my ear, his massive cock grinding on my belly. "Tell me what you want."

It's really fucking hard to concentrate while trying to control the uncontrollable, but I do. Because *he* asked me to. "Fuck my mouth, please."

"You want that, don't you?" His bite in my ear is swift and agonizing. I shriek. "Want to be filthy for me. Want to make me come."

"Yes."

"Yes." He nods in agreement.

Alistair straightens, grabbing a fistful of my hair to angle my head toward him. The minute I open up is the minute he shoves himself inside me, past my lips, my teeth, and down my throat.

"Fuck."

His groan reverberates through his body and his dick juts even deeper into my mouth. He leans his free hand on the headboard, beginning the slow rhythm of harsh thrusts.

"Look at me." There's no refusing his demand. My eyes snap up to him. "Keep being this good, Nola, and I'll let you come."

I know all too well what *being this good* means. Aside from hollowing my cheeks and letting him go deeper, I dig into myself to the hollow place in my heart, where pain, submission, and being owned are merged.

Where one emotion topples the other, where it's so overwhelming that my eyes tear up.

At the first sign of dampening in the corners of my eyes, his menacing voice turns approving. "My baby. That's it."

He pummels harder into me, his balls slapping to my saliva-coated chin. I gag on the sweet assault on my senses, and my lover grins.

"My sweet little student." He pauses, pulling himself out to free my airway. "Come for me."

Then he slams into me again. The moan I let out as I surrender to the vibrations on my pussy and Alistair's dick fucking my mouth isn't fully human.

Alistair reciprocates the sound coming out of me, and growls. I watch him, adoring him, licking, and sucking him.

I find immense pride and joy in being his human toy, but I continue to hurt. Another orgasm drums at my walls, behind my clit, between my ears. Coming now will involve a lot more pain than what I would endure from the torture of swallowing it down.

Alistair's probing stare communicates he's aware of the two tormenting options I'm facing. That he's getting off on it.

He drags his dick along my tongue, rests it on my cheek, and jerks himself off. "Come."

"No."

"Yes." His fingers drown deeper into the roots of my hair, pulling hard. "You'll come for me. And you'll do it when I say so."

I flail my body left and right, attempting to get rid of the damn vibrator. Alistair's knees lock me in, his hand pressing on my collarbone. A set of five fingers slide up to my throat, applying pressure on it.

"Whom do you breathe for?" he asks the question he likes to repeat.

The question I love answering. "You."

"Then you'll come for me." The pressure of his palm increases.

My labored breaths are accompanied by the never-ending buzzing sound. Suddenly, I don't hate it. I'm not in pain. I'm above all of it, thanks to the bliss that accompanies the reminder of being his.

"Do it."

Alistair doesn't promise me anything in return. Doesn't say he'll end it, that he'll spare me. Yet through the strength he transfers to me, channels into me, I realize it isn't necessary.

What matters is his ownership of me, this and this alone.

"Yes." I part my lips.

He returns to pummeling into my mouth. Our eyes lock, and I give him what he wanted: my agonizing, insides-tearing, brain-flipping orgasm. I cry out onto his shaft, choking and sucking on him in the interim.

"Gonna come, Nola." The grace of his thrusts wanes. He's an animal; pure unadulterated desire flows out of him in waves. "Swallow every fucking drop."

Without the ability to speak, I relax my jaw, even more, blinking at him once.

Warm spurts of his semen shoot into my mouth. His loud exhale lights my body up. My satisfaction from pleasing him doesn't compare to anything else I've achieved, worth the tears and the fear of another pending orgasm.

Which Alistair holds at bay. He fulfills his promise, kneeling at my side in a matter of seconds to switch off the wand and our scene with it.

His fingers are soft and caring as he undoes the ties and puts aside the wand. As he bends my knees to have my legs in the air, he removes the ribbons painlessly.

"Sweetheart," he murmurs, kissing the imprints of the tight knots left on my thighs as well as my sore, aching clit.

He then rolls me to the side, undoing the bow he tied around my wrists, and cradles me in his arms.

I'm loved and safe, not an inch less than I was during our scene, not an inch more.

I'm completely and hopelessly in love with him too, falling asleep to the echo of his voice.

Especially when he murmurs something about getting me my tea.

CHAPTER FIVE

Nora

"*Bon jour, Monsieur et Madame Cromwell,*" the concierge greets us in French.

While I'm not fluent, I don't speak over ten words on a good day, I understand the titles perfectly fine.

The independent woman might get pissed off. She might suggest that I correct Alistair's presumptuous ass to sign us under his surname.

Thing is, this woman is an idiot. Respectfully.

She would've read the room all wrong, would've missed how madly in love I am with Alistair.

I don't mind marrying him, as in, today. Whatever Vegas version France has to offer, sign me up.

But maybe Alistair didn't tell Hannah, his PA, to book us as Mr. and Mrs. Cromwell. Maybe it's an honest mistake on her part. That might be the case, and since I don't want to assume what isn't there, I keep my excitement to myself.

I glue my eyes to the white marble floor and its intricate gold vein embellishments, hoping my *husband* doesn't catch me blushing.

Alistair skips acknowledging the titles as well, getting me a little curious in the process. It's a question I probably won't be brave enough to ask, so I block it out, listening in on their conversation.

It's virtually impossible to catch a word here and there at the speed both men are speaking, but Alistair and his impeccable accent that send shivers down my spine with how sexy he is make up for what I can't understand. Another point to his advantage.

The concierge—Bernard, as Alistair called him—hands him two brown electronic tickets with gold lettering at the end of their conversation.

Alistair barely finishes thanking him when the bellboy who's waiting for us runs the cart with our luggage to the reserved elevators. Their dark wood covering looks pristine, like everything else in this hotel.

The sheer beauty, though, is dampened by a slight sense of unease that prods at my conscience. I'm about to tell Alistair he's overdone it—first the plane, now the hotel.

His hand slipping around my waist stops me dead in my tracks. The comfort, the warmth of it, the possessiveness. I succumb to his care, postponing this conversation for some other time.

At the top floor, the elevator stops and the bellboy gestures for us to step ahead of him.

Floor-to-ceiling windows are installed across the hallway, allowing the bright sunlight of the morning to seep in. The light casts on the potted fruit trees, the beige couches, and the lamps at the side of the walls, highlighting the colors of the gigantic paintings decorating it.

Our feet pace on identical marble tiles to the ones they have in the lobby as we're escorted to what seems to be the sole room on this floor.

"We were discussing the weather," Alistair whispers into my hair.

Yet again hindering my need to reproach him on how much this must've cost. With that small sentence, he surrenders me into a blubbering mess due to his insistence on not leaving me out of the earlier conversation.

"About new restaurants worth checking out." His fingers curl around my waist in his domineering fashion, dragging me to him. "And about how exquisitely beautiful you are."

"Oh, please." The heat in my cheeks can mean one thing, and one thing alone. I'm blushing.

Fuck.

"The last part isn't true." He releases me as the bellboy swipes the card on the key reader to open the door to our room. "I never leave a conversation with the other person thinking you're *just* beautiful. Everyone around me knows you're smart, talented, ambitious, queen of my…"

"That's enough." I elbow him. And laugh. The bellboy remains with his back to us, quietly pretending we don't exist as we speak.

Yeah, it's definitely expensive here.

"But you are." Alistair's smirk is audible.

"I get it."

"Everyone else should, as well," he drawls, then adds to my praise-loving self, "I'm so very proud of you. Even prouder to call you my girlfriend."

I notice the change in him. I really notice it. Around the time we met, Alistair wore his huge heart on his sleeve. To his employees—and there are plenty—by treating them with respect as equals, to my best friend Rhodes who worked at Toy Shop with me and who now helps me run We Love You when he called to ask for advice about me.

To everyone except me. He treated me like he'd treated his other temporary lovers since he didn't believe he was worthy of love. He held them all, including me, at arm's length.

So, to hear him getting sentimental on me, it's nothing short of an achievement for us as a couple. Getting him to love me is beside the point. It's his ability to love himself that takes up every occupied space in my heart.

"Thank you." I spin to face him, rising on my tiptoes and pressing my lips to his cheek. "Now, can we please relieve the poor man from listening to our PDA before we're late for our meeting?"

CHAPTER SIX
Nola

Alistair and I sit in the conference room of *Nous Sommes Rose*, We're Pink in French.

The family-owned sex toy company lives up to its name to the T—the cream-colored tablecloth around the oval table has pink embellishments, as do the curtains. The walls are painted in a dusty pink color to match a slightly lighter plush rug. Even our ceramic coffee cups have about a dozen tiny, adorable roses painted on them. In pink, of course.

I glance back at Alistair. He requested to attend the meeting as an observer, and I made him swear he wouldn't interrupt it, not for anything. And that's what he does. He believes I'm capable of holding it on my own, and so do I.

No, I don't speak the language. No, I'm not familiar with their customs. But I've done my research for the last few weeks since setting up the meeting with them. I browsed through thousands of other adult stores in the US to check what we have and don't have, and added an anonymous questionnaire to our clients to hear from them what they'd be interested in buying.

Regarding the costs involved, I'd say being my own boss for five whole months gave me a pretty good idea of what the price ranges should be.

I'm prepared, wearing the beige designer dress that hugs and molds over my curves and matching high-heeled boots.

Alistair purchased both for the occasion, which I didn't mind one bit. Firstly, because the dress hits me below my knees to hide the bruises—as if he had plans to smack the backs of my thighs in advance, the deviant.

Second, his habit has grown on me, this layer of our connection, to a certain limit. Like the day a stylist arrived carrying a whole new wardrobe to my apartment two months into our relationship.

A harmless dress here or a pair of jeans there, I kept quiet about. The relatively small purchases don't suffocate me or cause me to feel indebted to him.

I mean, who doesn't like her boyfriend's eyes heating and turning two shades darker whenever their gaze lands on them?

I do. Very much so.

And those are dirty, dirty thoughts I'll have to postpone for the evening.

For now, looking at Alistair is all I have. Sitting by the window, wearing an elegant blue suit and gray dress shirt since we're going out to lunch later and sipping on his tea, he's a dream.

Quiet.

Handsome.

The light streaming in through the curtains creates a game of shadows and highlights on his face. They accentuate the edges of his angular jaw and the sharp lines of his cheekbones.

He would've looked menacing if he hadn't sent me a wink.

Then the door creaks, announcing the arrival of Laurent and Delphine Rose.

CHAPTER SEVEN
Alistair

*S*omething stinks.

It isn't the sweetly sick scent of the colorful macarons on the table. It isn't the syrupy berries-scented diffuser placed on top of the decorative dressers on either side of the room either.

The room itself and the kind receptionist who welcomed us and showed us here, they're all right.

Our two hosts are my problem. There isn't anything I can pinpoint about what makes my jaw clench or my eyes narrow at them. This isn't something cultural; the sex toys I bought before I ordered from Nola's shop were bought in a sex shop in Paris.

I like the city, I love trailing the halls of the Louvre. I could eat their *duck à l'orange* for dinner for the rest of my days.

Nothing against the French. On the contrary. Just these two.

"Bon jour, Madame Vickers," both of them chime in tandem.

The years of entrepreneurship experience I have under my belt and the dozens of scumbags I've come across have sharpened my senses. And these senses fucking scream at me to wake up as Laurent kisses the back of Nola's palm and his sister, Delphine kisses her cheeks from either side.

I. Do. Not. Like them.

But I promised Nola I'd be a wallflower at her meeting, and I'll honor my word. Our relationship is based on mutual respect, on honoring each other. The fact that she even agreed to let me in on it—so I could witness her in her element—attests to the deep level of trust we've built.

A hunch will not trigger me to break it. It'll take a hell of a lot more than that.

"Bon jour, Monsieur et Madame Rose," my Nola does her best impression of Bernard.

I temporarily forget about my dislike of the Rose siblings at the nearly perfect French accent she's adopted in the past two hours we've been here.

"*Mon Dieu!*" Delphine coos at her. "*Est-ce que tu parles Français?*"

"No, no." Nola chuckles. "I don't speak French."

From my vantage point at her side, I watch the nearly undetectable clenching of her fists at her sides.

She's doing a damn good job at masking her inexperience.

She reminds me of myself. My first few official meetings to raise money for SunInUs, the solar panel company I built with my own two hands, were brutal.

I was twenty-three years old, grief-laden by the death of my sister and my parents not long after her. They died within one week of each other, their personal grief for their daughter's early demise taking them from me and my other sister, Jolene.

I was poor as shit, too. Not a penny from their life policy entered my bank account. The blame for all of their deaths is mine, alone. Leaving the money to Jolene was the least I could do as penance, an insignificant atonement for my sins. One I continue paying, despite her pleas to stop.

But I digress.

Throughout the internal shitstorm that wreaked havoc in me, I still showed up at the meetings, put up a straight, strong face, and charged forward, taking no prisoners.

Similar to my Nola.

"Well, your accent is flawless," Delphine continues, her smile widening. "Isn't it, Laurent?"

"*Oui, oui.*" He nods emphatically.

They seem too nice. Too eager. Maybe they recognize me? It's not entirely impossible, my face has appeared in global magazines, and I've been at it for a while. Maybe they want to be cordial.

Maybe I'm being a jerk for being unable to shake off this unexplained repugnance for them.

"Who is this gentleman?" Delphine turns to me.

I stay silent, adamant to let Nola navigate through the situation.

"This is my boyfriend." Nola's face shines at me. "Alistair Cromwell. We're visiting together and he asked to tag along." She looks back at the siblings. "I hope you don't mind."

"Not at all." Laurent approaches me first, shaking my hand. "This is a family-operated company. We welcome and encourage, whether it be with our employees, clients, or suppliers."

Delphine outstretches her hand after him, which I shake. "Indeed. We're very happy to have you here, Monsieur Cromwell."

"Thank you, but this isn't about me." I return to my seat, scooting it another inch until it hits the wall.

Invisible.

For the next thirty minutes, they show Nola new lines of products they haven't revealed to any of their other clients. They claim they were completely besotted by her ambition, her all-inclusive shop, and the great reviews she received online, that they're happy to sign exclusivity in the US and are excited about their future endeavors.

Nola holds onto her poker face, smiling and sobering at the right time. But most of all, she's listening. She feels the vibrators they show her, the anal beads, the sex card games, cuffs, and floggers.

She's pleased. They're pleased.

Maybe I was wrong.

"We hit a gold mine here," Delphine says to her brother in French while Nola tests the speeds and sound levels of a crocodile-shaped vibrator.

The hairs at the back of my neck stand on end. My heartbeat races. My muscles tense.

Ready to pounce.

"She has no idea," Laurent agrees.

"No idea whatsoever. The poor sap." She nods to the unsuspecting Nola who tells her she likes the glow-in-the-dark vibrator as well. "People from around here, they know how much it costs us, give or take. If in America it's the norm to pay more…"

"Then we'll take it."

They're not whispering, trying to make it sound like any normal, daily conversation between two family members.

Me, on the other hand, I'm not smiling at all. I'm hanging by a thread, and yet I need to keep my cool. This is Nola's moment. Nola's decisions. Running a business entails stumbling, getting shit wrong, accepting it as a learning experience, moving on stronger.

But Nola isn't by herself. She has me.

My responsibility for her runs deeper than capturing and releasing her breath. It's more profound than the fucking tea I have set for her after sex.

It's about protecting her. Looking after her.

Allowing no one, not a fucking soul, to disrespect her.

Myself, included. Because even though these two are the scum of the earth, it's her meeting. And she'll be the one to lay it into them.

"Nola." My strained voice catches her attention.

"Alistair?" She tilts her head.

What she meets is the mien of fury I'm tamping down to the best of my abilities.

For her.

"Outside."

"What?"

I rise to my feet. Three sets of eyes look at me. Two are curious, one is worried.

Plastering a forced smile on my face, I place a hand on Nola's shoulder. "Nola, if you will."

"Okay." She sees I'm not backing down, my decision set in stone. "Delphine, Laurent, I'm so sorry about this. We'll be back in a second."

"No worries, take your time." The bitch waves at us, delighted.

Why wouldn't she wait? She's got hours to spend on her cash cow.

My blood runs hotter at the idea.

"Alistair, what happened?"

"Come with me, please." I'm aware of my Southern accent slipping. I can't fucking help how pissed I am.

I rest a hand on her back, scurrying her away from prying eyes to the direction of the bathroom.

Under no circumstance do I want any of them saying her older boyfriend instructed her on how to run her business. No matter how badly I'm keen to threaten, raise my voice, or burn down this company.

This should be and would be one hundred percent Nola. Whichever way she chooses to use the information I'm handing her, the couple of people who work during the Christmas–New Year's vacation won't gossip about Nola being manhandled.

We enter the women's toilet. The tiles on the walls here are consistent with the brand—pink, like the doors to the stalls, like the rosy scent permeating the air. It's nauseating, but their design choice isn't my main concern at the moment.

Nola is.

I close the door to the whole restroom, lock it, and turn to her.

"What are you doing?" she seethes.

Her fists are clenched, red spots burst on her cheeks. Deep down, she must know I'd never embarrass her. She just doesn't see it yet.

I launch into my explanation, "You shouldn't be doing business with these people."

"You promised you wouldn't intervene," she blurts the words out fast. "You promised you wouldn't patronize me."

Conflicted between the urge to pacify her and the anger at the Rose family, my answer comes out as a harsh, "No."

"No, what?" Nola advances at me.

She should be pissed. She should be fuming. Instead, she's furrowing her brow, searching my face with every step she takes forward. I need to give her answers.

"'No,' you didn't promise? 'No,' you didn't mean to intervene?"

She's so close now, she cranes her neck to look at me. What a wonderful creation of God she is. I marvel at the force she emanates, her gleaming brown eyes, her full set of lips.

As an owner of a large conglomerate, one of the aspects of my job is to put out fires. Every major scale problem finds itself on my desk, and it's expected of me to fix it. Not in this case—she won't let me. I won't let myself.

The helplessness of it all leaves me stumped.

For a moment.

I grab her by the shoulders, spinning her so her back is against the wall.

"No, as in you're not listening." My fingers locate her tender neck. "No, as in I'm not patronizing you."

Her pulse thrums beneath my finger pads. Slow, steady, and so fucking strong. She's listening to me.

My eyes connect with hers. We're both spitting fire, swirling and entwining in an uncontrollable blaze of wrath and desire.

"No,"—I press my forehead to hers, reveling in her staccato breaths. Dipping my free hand into a jacket pocket, I extract what I planned to put to good use after our lunch—"you don't get how much your Daddy cares for you. And if you need proof, I'm more than happy to demonstrate it."

CHAPTER EIGHT
Nora

"Spread your legs."

Alistair's lips barely brush mine, cautious not to ruin my lipstick. He applies an identical harsh-thoughtful nipping at my jaw—doesn't bite, doesn't suck. Doesn't leave marks.

It's a challenge to reconcile his care now with the man who—even when done elegantly—dragged me out of a meeting. *My* meeting.

He swore he'd be a bystander, a delicate wallflower. Him and his full one-eighty pounds of pure muscle in an expensive suit. He promised.

I scan his eyes, searching for the answer as to why he went back on his word. There has to be one. I need to believe it, that he didn't veto my business just because.

It has to be there, hidden beneath his silence.

But he gives me nothing. His half-longing, half-raging eyes exude his control of me. I'm not curious anymore. I'm mad. His promise is off the table, and so is my submission.

"No." It's my turn to refuse him. My temper rises at the sight of the glass butt plug in his hand next to his pants pocket. "Tell me what was so fucking wrong that we're here. Doing this, instead of me signing the deal for my shop."

"My Nolita." He tugs my skirt up.

I push it down. "Don't fuck me. Not when we're talking boundaries, Alistair."

"I didn't intend to." His head angles up to meet me, his dark gaze morphing into a deadly shade of black. "However, I'm beginning to worry you won't listen."

My lips scrunch in my attempt to calm myself, to annihilate the imminent wave of tears. In these short five months of our relationship, Alistair has unearthed parts of my personality I didn't know existed. He's studied them, analyzed them.

The erudite man he is, he applies his mental dissection of me to read me better than my own parents do.

He's right.

Despite questioning him, despite my brain demanding logical answers, my heart isn't in it.

In the conference room, I was already crossing the finish line. I envisioned these new high-quality products in my shop, the sales I'd run often to make them accessible to a wider crowd. Rhodes would've loved these. He would've shared my enthusiasm. He would've approved.

Whatever Alistair would've said, at my heightened level of eagerness, would've been shut down. In the present moment, though, as he pushes the butt plug on my chin, my focus and trust return to him. To listen.

"Spit."

I don't bother turning him down or demand he explain this very minute. I'm in Alistair's world, cognizant that whatever he says or does is for me.

I spit.

"Very good."

Someone presses down the door handle on the outside, rattling it in an attempt to figure out why it won't open.

"Occupied," Alistair thunders.

A rush of French expels from the other side of the wall, accompanied by loud banging.

Alistair replies in his calm and frightening tone.

The woman on the outside quiets, then the heels of her boots click toward the distance.

With my attention fixed on his mouth, uncontrollably aroused by his French, I failed to notice him lifting my leg to round his waist and his deft fingers parting my folds.

The wet tip of the butt plug in my ass wakes me up.

"Hold your leg up."

"Okay." I do, and he frees his hand to rub my clit.

"I told her you're pumping milk." He supplies an answer I haven't asked for. Even during the emotional rollercoaster we're on, he doesn't let me feel left out. "That if she embarrasses you by telling anyone, I'll bring her lack of humanity to the attention of her bosses."

"Oh, my God—" The rest of my sentence is *You're the worst.* Supposed to be, anyway.

Alistair's fingers extract the wetness from my pussy, dragging it down to my pucker. The tip of the butt plug makes way for Alistair's middle finger to penetrate me, to lube my ass in slow thrusts.

"Oh, my God," I repeat, banging my head on the wall.

"Do you need your safeword?"

It sounds like a simple question. What he's really asking is, *Do you want to do this, here and now? Are you ready to listen? Will you take what I give you like a good little girl?*

"No, so long as we do it fast."

The side of his lips quirks up. "As you wish, sweetheart."

His words float in the air while the butt plug plunges into my ass in a swift, circular motion. I claw at Alistair's jacket, biting my bottom lip to restrain a scream. He's quick to free his cock, even quicker to ram it into my pussy.

I balance on a thin heel; my back is hammered into the wall. My insides are unstable as well. Alistair executes his reign over me, his hand at my nape commanding me as his.

"Are you ready to listen to what they said?"

His glare requires me to tell him and myself the truth. Looking deep inside for whether I'm ready or not isn't necessary anymore.

I'm Alistair's. I'm Daddy's. Each of his strokes reaffirms what I already know and should never forget: I'm his number one priority. I always ought to, at the very least, carve space in my heart to hear him out.

"I…" The base of his cock slams against my cunt. "Do."

"They're ripping you off." His measured rocking in and out of me runs slower and somehow deeper. "They offer the French one at a lower price. To you, they created a personal, higher price list. They're happy to screw you over."

My lust-filled brain rewinds itself to the meeting. I chalked off their conversations in French to casual, family talk. I avoided being rude by not staring at them. Didn't so much as suspect.

The icing on the cake though, the height of my stupidity, is doubting Alistair. It shouldn't have taken me forever to realize that he might've picked up on something I couldn't.

"None of this." His voice is in my ear, his fingers searing into my fresh bruises. "You haven't done anything wrong. Not your beautiful heart,"—he dips his lips to my chest, kissing it—"not your calculated brain."

He kisses my temple, and fucks and fucks and fucks my worries away.

The pain and pleasure, his rough version of affection and mounds of unyielding concern, they surround me. Engulf me.

I stop hating myself.

Love steps into the space self-reproach vacated— for Alistair, for me, for us.

"I'm coming."

It's a plea. The need for his approval, at this point in time, tops the all-consuming orgasm. I just *need* to be told I please him.

A blessing he doesn't hesitate to give me.

"My fierce, valiant queen." His scruff tickles my jaw, his lips ghosting my cheek. "Yes."

White-hot light blinds me, purifies me. It radiates throughout my body, taking shape and form and suddenly it's a man. Alistair shines brightly before me.

I grasp the small hairs of his nape, dragging his face to mine.

Fuck my lipstick.

I pull him that extra inch, crushing our lips together. His orgasm blends with my own, electrifying the both of us. I feel it in my mouth through his groan, in his chest through labored breaths.

Where we connect, his thick semen unloads into me in three explosive shots.

"Nola." His large palm caresses my cheek, his other one helps settle me back to standing on my own two feet.

"I love you, Alistair."

"And I, you."

CHAPTER NINE
Nora

Alistair removes the butt plug slowly. After cleaning it in the vanity and tucking himself in, he prepares me two wet washcloths.

One, he dabs at my center before rearranging my underwear back in place, then runs it along the inside of my thighs. The other, he pats on the corners of my mouth for the smeared lipstick.

"All done." After disposing of both, he returns to me. His eyes study mine, his hands are clasped together. "So."

A knock interrupts us. Alistair ignores it completely.

"What's the plan?"

"I need more details to make an educated decision." I smooth my messy hair down, picking up the speed of my speech. "What exactly did they say?"

Alistair beams at me. This isn't a smirk, not at all. It's a look of contentment.

He's proud of how I am choosing to handle it.

"As I said, they boasted about how the prices to manufacture sex toys here are lower."

The redness of exertion on his cheeks dissolves. Other than an unruly strand of hair and his slightly crumpled suit jacket, no one would ever imagine this somber man just finished drilling me into the bathroom wall.

"I deduced from what they said that their local clients can estimate what each product should cost like you're aware of those of your suppliers back home. My bet is, the Rose family managed to get their hands on the US prices. They can't charge it to their old clientele, or they'll leave them. They can, however, will ask *and* receive it from unsuspecting clients overseas."

He notices my fallen expression, gripping my chin to tilt my head up.

"Nola, you're still brand new to this world, it's a wonder your shop is turning profits, as is. I'm so proud of you. You can't blame yourself for them giving you a false picture of what the market here is like, or for laughing about it. Not. Your. Fault." And then his signature smirk arrives. "I'll fuck your cunt, ass, and mouth a million times over until you get it into your head."

"The part about it not being my fault is clear." I sigh. "It's just… Do I even have the right to be upset? Isn't it their right to charge anything they want? Free market and all?"

"It's not about the prices. It's a matter of respect. If anyone talked shit about me,"—his nostrils flare—"looked down on me. Would you allow it?"

The mere thought sparks my immediate fury. "I would've punched their fucking throats."

"Remind me not to mess with you." Alistair chuckles, shaking his head.

"I'm not doing business with them." I come to the inevitable conclusion. My shoulders slump, disappointment dampens my eyes. "At least we gained a New Year's trip out of it, right?"

"Maybe all isn't lost."

An abundance of scenarios play in my head, none are viable. There's no one I know here, no friends or business connections. No one will read their emails on what should be a national holiday.

"Would you be willing to hear a solution I might have?" His gaze dances across the bathroom. "Outside of here?"

This day brought the realization that having Alistair's input, even when I don't straight up ask him of it, doesn't take away from me being a boss lady.

He proved I can trust him not to treat me like a little girl, to stay beside me, never ahead. It showed in his rage in that conference room. His outward kindness was nonexistent, and yet he sucked it up. Said nothing until we were out of earshot.

Respected me.

My ovaries demand that I hug him for that fact, alone.

My heart commands me to do it later, trust him now.

Any suggestion he brings to the table, he'll do to empower me. He'll leave it to my final judgment. I can get behind that.

"Yes. Absolutely yes." I clutch onto his suit jacket lapels, tugging him to me for a quick kiss. "Soon. There's something I have to do before we leave. I have some unfinished business."

The sadist in him awakens. His eyes darken, his white teeth flash like the predator he is.

"After you." He unlocks the door to the bathroom, clearing the path for me.

The sound of my clicking heels reverberates in Rose's halls. Alistair falls into step with me, once again opening the door to the conference room.

"Nola, Alistair." Delphine rises, the money-hungry smile glued to her lips. "We were starting to get worried."

Alistair closes the door, staying put while I face them.

These two people believed they could mock me for my naïveté, gossip about me to my face for not speaking their language.

They underestimated me and the power of my relationship.

For that, they'll pay.

"It's Ms. Vickers, to you." I glower at her.

"I apologize, I don't think I understand?" Her joyful demeanor wanes.

Her brother appears at her side. A united family front.

What a joke. Like these two intimidate me. A) The mask hiding their asshole-ness has been lifted, so honestly, their theatrics look more pathetic than anything. B) The throbbing pain in the back of my thighs and ass reminds me of what I've taken, how I've endured, and tells me what a piece of fucking cake this should be.

"First thing's first: I am not going into business with you."

"Your boyfriend has another supplier, correct?" Laurent asks. "He's been hostile since the start."

"You want to know why Alistair has been hostile?" My eyes narrow. I erect my spine to all of my five-foot-seven inches, plus the other two and a half from my boots. "Alistair is fluent in French."

Delphine gasps.

"Yes." I let that sink in, sidestepping them to grab my bag and our coats. "Good luck with finding any other client in the States. I'll make sure to spread the word that the Rose family considers us idiots. I'm confident many sex shop owners will find that attitude highly unappealing."

"We apologize." Laurent lifts his hands in surrender. "Please, you can't do that."

"Watch me."

I glance at Alistair from across the desk. His eyes glimmer, his chest is puffed.

His silent praise encourages me to take that final step. I swipe the contract they almost had me sign off the table, tearing it into smithereens. The paper shreds fall like snow to the floor.

Now, I'm done.

Alistair holds the door for me, and we're out.

Only in the elevator do we speak again.

"How are you?" He tucks a wayward lock of hair behind my ear.

"Not the happiest." I snuggle into his raised arm, the invitation for a side embrace. "I was really looking forward to it. They had great toys, too."

The elevator pings, announcing our arrival on the ground floor of the building. We exit to the snowy sidewalk, where Alistair holds me to help me balance while still rushing forward.

The driver Alistair rented for the trip tips his hat and opens the back of the Bentley for us. We climb inside, and Alistair tells him something in French.

He starts the car, blasting the heater on. I expect him to roll into the road toward the restaurant we had booked for lunch, but he doesn't move.

"About my proposition."

Oh, so that's what he told him. To hang on and wait for my choice.

"I'm all ears."

"Julia, the woman who owned the sex shop I used to buy from, she left me the number of the boutique factory where she bought her inventory."

My mouth opens to ask a question that my brain finds the answer to quickly. "You haven't mentioned it the entire time because you didn't want to meddle."

"That's correct." He rubs my covered knee. His palm is cold even through the fabric, his gaze, is fiery hot. "I haven't talked to them. There's no backup plan, whatsoever. But if you like them, I'm pretty convinced a call from Julia could land us a meeting."

"Really?" My squeaky voice fills the car. I leap on Alistair, enveloping his broad shoulders and even bigger heart in my arms. "Holy shit, that'd be awesome. Thank you. Thank you so much."

His rumbling chuckle rings beautifully in my ears. "Hold your horses. You haven't even looked at their catalog."

I pull back, my mouth forming an O shape. "You have it here?"

"Julia sent me everything I might need." He presses a finger to the bottom of my chin, snapping my mouth shut with amusement dancing in his eyes. "I was one of her favorite clients, and she was aware of my busy schedule. She tried to spare me the pain of going back and forth, in case I didn't find anything fitting in the US. Which I have."

Roger's shop, my former workplace, springs to mind. I cock an eyebrow. "You haven't."

"I'm not talking about the products. I'm talking about you."

"Alistair…"

"It's getting late, a day before New Year's." He clears a tear I hadn't felt sliding down my cheek. "Come take a look at their catalog, see if it's something you'd like for your shop. You do—I'll make the call to have Julia convince them to meet us this afternoon."

"Or we could stay another week."

"I would've called you greedy." Alistair's lips tilt to the side as he browses his phone. "Thing is, I'm willing to bet every business I own that you're more eager to return to work than I am."

As always, Alistair is right.

CHAPTER TEN
Alistair

The meeting with Avryll, the owner of the sex toy factory, took place around five hours after the morning's debacle. She had family matters, which left Nola and me to enjoy our lunch and explore the city.

We drove through Paris, getting out of the car to observe the river Seine, Place de la Concorde, Montmartre, and many other impressive monuments and snowy gardens of the city.

They were fun to watch, especially through Nola's eyes, who saw everything for the first time. Her awe, her giddiness. She'd been effervescent in her enthusiasm, sucking me into marveling at them anew alongside her.

But what was exponentially more enjoyable, was sitting in on her successful meeting with Avryll later. The successful one.

The one Nola nailed.

Not thanks to me, obviously. I did nothing except sit quietly by her side in the booth the three of us occupied and listened in. The pastry shop down the street from Avryll's apartment wasn't busy, but it was still nice to have our corner for Nola to examine Avryll's toys and talk business.

During their negotiations, I noticed Avryll's prices were fairly lower than Nous Somme Rose's. The reason they weren't lower was due to Nola's insistence on exclusivity, a factor Avryll calculated, fairly, into the final price offer.

But my fondness of her wasn't just about her being fair to my Nola.

Avryll treated my girlfriend with genuine kindness and respect, as Nola deserved. It tugged at my heartstrings, the ability to offer Nola the opportunity of a fair meeting those bastards denied her.

I hoped while looking at her artwork of a profile, that if everything went according to plan, she'd enable me to give her plenty of others in the future.

Once everything is sorted out, I—to Nola and Avryll's protests—pay the check. We unfold ourselves from the booth, heading to the front of the pastry shop.

Avryll puts on her gloves, coat, and woolen hat in the coat room. "It's been lovely meeting you, the both of you."

"Thank you for carving out time out of your holiday for us." Nola accepts the coat I hold for her, slipping one hand in after the other. "We truly appreciate it."

"We do," I acquiesce.

"Don't even mention it." She picks up her bulky, leather suitcase off the floor.

Nola mirrors her movement, lifting a bag of her own from the floor. A large, pastel-yellow bag that says *Avryll's* in amethyst script lettering. The Christmas spirit and the women's burgeoning friendship have put Avryll in a giving mood, and despite Nola's unease with receiving gifts, she accepts them.

"Our ride is right outside." I gesture to the street where the Bentley awaits.

Snowflakes pour from the sky, white prisms on a dark, cloudy night. Our evening meeting has slipped well into the late hours, and it seems rude that we send Avryll off by herself.

"I insist you let us take you home. It's the least we can do."

"No, no." She lifts her scarf to her nose, her green eyes smiling at Nola, then at me. "I've been sitting for far too long. I could use the walk."

"You sure?" Nola asks, sounding way too upbeat for someone who's been up for so many hours, plus the jet lag.

I gaze at her wide eyes, her effervescent smile. Energy whirrs and buzzes around her slender frame in a sphere.

Earlier, I might've contributed it to the signing.

Now that we're about to be left alone to play, I know better.

"Oui," Avryll replies. Without giving us another chance to argue, she spins on her heels, rushing out into the night.

"You have plans for us." I drape my coat on top of Nola's head.

The walk to the car is short—I won't miss it, won't freeze to death during the two minutes there. Nola, on the other hand, is mine to protect for even half a step in snowy weather.

"Is that an issue?"

I climb into the car after her, engulfing Nola in the warmth of my body. My lips lower to her ear, nuzzling my nose to her hair.

She giggles and shifts as my cold mouth meets her ear, and I suck her scent in. It's partly her flowery fragrance, partly the crisp winter. I embed it into my head, as I do the curve of her thigh with my palm.

"The only issue I have is being unable to teleport us into the hotel room." I snake my hand between her thighs, cupping her cunt above her dress.

Or that you might stumble upon the gift I'm saving for your surprise tomorrow.

The ring is hidden in a compartment in my suitcase, where it should stay until tomorrow night. Thing is, ever since I told Nola about my sister's passing, we've held no secrets from each other. We have an open channel of communication twenty-four seven and because she's practically moved into my house, all my rooms are available for her to browse through.

There isn't a drawer in my home I keep locked, no secret stashed in my metaphorical attic.

It isn't far-fetched that she'd go through my suitcase for a shirt she'll want to sleep in and find a bump in the shape of a silk box. I have zero control over it. I just have to pray she won't. Like I pray for her—the love of my life, the woman I never thought I'd deserve but secretly wished for—to say yes.

"I bet you'll come up with a solution for both."

"There's nothing, absolutely nothing,"—I take her chin between my fingers, lowering my face until our noses meet—"I won't do for you."

Nola's hand explores the length of my thigh, trailing up and down, sending bolts of fire throughout me whenever her hand brushes my balls or her thumb strokes the base of my shaft.

I grip her shoulder as a warning. She ignores it altogether.

She twists her head, whispering to me, "You're so good to me, Daddy."

"Not for long," I grit out.

"So caring." Her hand courses up my hardening dick, squeezing and rubbing it the way she knows drives me crazy. "So loving. So. Fucking. Hot."

The driver pulls over. I tear my eyes from Nola's neck, against my steadfast wish to bite it, and look outside.

The Haussmann-style building, the orange glow of the lobby, the bare, lit trees flanking the entrance.

Our hotel.

When the door opens, I don't waste a single moment. I pull the coat over Nola's head again, take the yellow bag in one hand, gripping Nola's in the other.

"You're free for the night. See you tomorrow evening." I thank our driver and stalk off with my woman.

"We're not doing any more sightseeing in the morning?" Teasing lingers in her voice.

"We will. In the evening." We walk briskly past the concierge straight to the old elevators. The bellboy jogs toward us. I shake my head subtly in a *No, thanks* gesture.

"After you catch up on some sleep hours and rest." I pin her to the ascending elevator's wall, grinding my body to hers. My palm rounds her jaw, angling her head up, and I nip at her bottom lip.

"Because tonight, sweetheart, you're not getting either."

I catch her gasp with my mouth, devouring her in a long, punishing kiss. We battle one another until the elevator's melodic *ping* clamors.

Waiting for her ceases to be a viable option. I shift the bag up my arm, hoisting Nola up, and slinging her over my shoulder. Her laughter shakes her soft belly. Feeling it is as much of a turn-on as listening to her melodic giggles.

But there's nothing like her gasps.

My palm lands on her ass in a sharp *thump* that echoes in our private hallway, and she grunts. There's such a satisfaction to it, to have her under my complete and utter mercy, whimpering in pain, that I do it twice more.

"Again," she moans.

Inside our room, I kick the door back. I peel up Nola's skirt and bite her ass on my walk to the bed, sucking and tormenting the tender piece of flesh without faltering.

"Greedy girl." I traverse past the suite's expansive living room on its farmhouse rug, careful not to bump into the antique wood tables and sofas.

The soundtrack of Nola's half-yelps, half-moans beats having Beethoven playing in the background, and my constant afflictions ensure she sings to me all the way to the four-poster bed.

"You'll only ask for something when I give you permission to speak your mind." I toss Nola onto the bed. The mattress's springs creak at the same time the air heaves out of Nola's lungs.

"Unless you're okay with not getting what you want." I furrow my brow meaningfully. "I won't repeat myself."

Nola pushes off the coat I had on her, biting her bottom lip, playful and tempting all at once. "Yes, Daddy."

God-fucking-dammit. I almost drop on one knee then and there to ask her to be my wife. But I rein it in.

"That's better." I curl my fingers around her wrist, pull her up to tear off her coat, and twist her to face the other side of the room.

I tug on her hair, moving it away to clear the left side of her neck. My lips are at the shoulder I've been fantasizing about, my free hand lowering the zipper of her dress to where the crack of her ass begins.

With one last bite of her skin, I release Nola altogether and take a step back.

"Out of that dress. Now."

Nola obeys, staring me in the eye. Her hand goes under one short sleeve, shoving it down her arm. The other follows. The beige fabric slides down her curves, bunching at her boots.

Her beige lace bra leaves very little to the imagination. Soft, round mounds are squeezed out of the demi cups, and pert nipples poke beneath them.

My gaze skates to her matching panties, to the mess I left them in. The waistline is scrunched, the wet crotch clings to her folds. The dark, wet line in the center of her panties is recent. It's fucking mouthwatering.

One heel at a time, she spreads her toned legs. I nod in appreciation, while the rest of me holds still as a statue. I don't bother looking at her, shrugging one shoulder and pretending her arousal didn't just make my balls tighten.

"Do I please you?"

"Your boots." I jerk my chin toward them. "Bend over for me and take them off."

She turns, giving me a view of her ass, unable to see me extracting the crop paddle whip out of Avryll's bag. It's much smaller than ours, a deliverer of a sting rather than a thudding sensation. Perfect for the current state of Nola's behind.

I approach her, launching short, calculated spanks on her mildly-reddened thighs.

Right thigh, left thigh, and again.

She lets out this choked sound that has me fisting my cock. Another two higher toward her ass, and Nola stops altogether.

"What do we have here?"

"I… Oh…" *Snap, snap* where her ass meets her thigh. "It's so good, Alistair."

"Does it seem like I care?"

Another string of softer smacks on her bottom coaxes suffocated sounds of desire out of her.

Each of my words has a swat accompanying it. "What. Did. I. Tell. You. To. Do?"

"My boots." She's breathing hard. "You said to take them off."

I yank her panties to the middle of her thighs, gliding my fingers over her dripping slit.

"That's right." The small paddle strikes at the top of her crack. She makes a guttural sound, and my cock jerks in my pants. "And what is it that you're doing?"

"I'm trying."

A clear drop slips down her cunt, her desire dampening her inner thigh. She clutches on the zipper of her boot, giving it another go.

I watch. I'm patient.

But it's not kindness dictating my mood.

My other plans for Nola do.

CHAPTER ELEVEN
Nora

"On your back," Alistair growls.

The low sting of the paddle emphasizes his request. It pats my exposed pussy at a tempo that causes my legs to quiver.

I obey by placing one knee on the bed, starting to turn while grappling with the roaring lust which slows my process.

"Faster." My sweet sadist smacks the leather surface on my waist, the side of my breast, my nipple.

"I'm trying," I whine a second time, even though I know it'll bring more pain. Maybe because of it.

And I get what I want. *Smack, smack, smack.* One of my breasts flares in a tingling sensation, then the other.

Alistair pushes his body weight on top of me, slithering the paddle to my navel. "Be my good little girl, Nola. Try. Harder."

His tone is harsher than any whip, softer than the fluffiest cloud.

Alistair is love.

Seeing my legs locked by my panties and Alistair's pressure on me, my twist to my back is far from elegant. I collapse on it, a toy for Alistair's pleasure.

"Beautiful girl," he muses, entangling our brown eyes in a sensual bind. "Beautiful, beautiful girl."

The longer he looks at me, assessing his next move, the faster my pulse goes. Alistair stands there in all his glory, his full dark-blond hair, the breadth of his shoulders. The thick member in his pants.

Even in this delicate room—contrary to his clean, modern home—Alistair doesn't lose an ounce of the brutal force his body emanates.

This impressive statue of a man moves, starts by removing my boots and socks. My panties come off next.

"Part your knees to the sides." Arousal coats the words he drawls out of his sinister mouth.

The vulnerability of lying there bare naked while he's fully dressed doesn't put me at a disadvantage. It sets the mood for our dark sex games. I do as he asks.

"I can see your pink, taut clit." He brings my panties to his nose, sniffing them. "Fuck. Feel up that little nub, baby. Touch yourself for Daddy."

His lust and filthy mouth spike my ravenous need for him, burning me, incinerating me to the ground. He doesn't have to provide me with any further incentive to do as he says. I just do it.

"Pinch it. Pull on it." His eyes are hooded, his speech slow and sensual. "Make it hurt."

He's never given me that kind of power. Alistair prefers to hold onto control, inflicting the pain himself. It's the second time he's gone out of character on this trip.

But now I already anticipate his response, how temporary the power shift will be.

I follow his orders, anxious to see where they'll lead us. I squirm at the pain of twisting and pulling on my clit, sucking my lips in. It hurts. It arouses me. Though it's nowhere near the heights I experience under Alistair's physical torture.

"See, that's not what I asked." He tsks.

Alistair discards my panties, throwing the paddle at his side to the nearest wall. With the force he applies to it, even though the instrument is light, the crash is audible.

"What I asked"—he meanders to the bag on the rug, returning to the edge of the bed with a black plastic box—"is for you to make it *hurt*."

"It did."

I don't argue to prove him wrong; I argue to egg him on and get to the fun parts faster.

"Since you didn't follow my instructions." He quirks an eyebrow as if his X-ray eyes see right into my very soul. "I'll have to do it myself."

All while he talks, his hands are busy snapping the box open. He removes the metallic rose gold nipple clamps from it. The metallic chain connecting the adjustable alligator clamps glints in the light of the lamp behind me. A threat as well as a promise.

Then Alistair climbs on top of me, menacing and hot. "Hands up, sweetheart."

The cold chain lies on my skin until I do it. His hands work me, one tweaking my erect nipple, making it even harder. I groan and moan, panting at the intense methods he uses to arouse me.

"Stay still."

He slides the black plastic parts of the clamps to clasp around my nipple. The screw-pin turns between his fingers, enhancing the crimping sensation on my nub.

"Nola." His tone is smooth, his words are too. Just for this brief moment. "If at any time your nipples go numb, you tell me. You hear? I won't enjoy this evening a fraction less if you said your safeword at any point."

"I'll say red."

"Good girl."

He resumes adjusting the clips. His brow furrows, his concentration ever so sexy. I raise my hips, seeking the barest friction. None of the strong features of his face twitch when he pins me back to the mattress.

"Alistair."

"What did I say?" His methods of rousing my other nipple are harsher—smacking, twisting it between punishing fingers. "Not a single word."

The other clamp is adjusted to my nipple. The metal of the chain begins to adjust to my body heat. A steady pulse drums from my nipples across my body, and the word *please* aches to leave my lips.

Alistair studies me a second longer. I give him nothing.

Nodding, he gets up to walk to the sofa behind him. He drapes his suit jacket on it, turning back to me, rolling up his sleeves, revealing strong, veiny forearms.

"These aren't the only clamps Avryll surprised you with."

I shake my head.

He lowers to retrieve a bottle of warming lube and another box from the bag. This one is long and rectangular and I can see through the box. I gauge the clit clamp sitting inside it, as the toy we haven't used yet, swallowing hard.

"That fear." The ruler of my heart crawls back up holding the device in his hand. "It belongs to me. You know why?"

"Why?"

The rubber tip of the clamp slips across my bottom lip. Alistair lets the clamp pinch it, then tugs on it, revealing my bottom gums.

"Because you're mine. I'm the one who delivers your pain with care. I'm the one who drives pleasure into this beautiful soul. You're my love, my soulmate. No one, not one person in this entire fucking universe will take you and this from me."

My eyes tear up. Equal, intense, and out-of-this-world love reflects from me too.

"I don't think you'll ever get what your tears do to me." He releases my lip, probing the device into my mouth. "Now, open up. Give me your tongue."

The slight panic taking over me must show on my face like an SOS sign.

"Never gonna cause you damage, Nola," he reassures me, knowing I feared him clamping my tongue.

And I believe him. My tongue darts out, accepting the clamp into my mouth. The rubbery taste should disgust me, but it doesn't. Gazing up at Alistair, at his darkened eyes, I'm eager to do anything.

"Suck on it." The top of the clamp presses onto my tongue a little tighter. "When it locks down on your pussy, I want your spit and mine on it. As if the both of us are kissing your clit. Together."

It's so fucking dirty, but God, does it turn me on. My skin prickles all over, and I suck on the clamp enthusiastically. A minute, two, or an eternity pass while he looks deep into my eyes and I use all the saliva within me to dampen the new toy.

"That's enough." He pulls it out, drawing back from me.

I miss his warmth the second he's gone.

Thankfully, he doesn't leave me wanting for long.

He closes the clamp on the chain of the nipple clamps, lowering himself to the bed. His mouth is on my aching mound, fulfilling his promise to have his saliva on it too. He's straining my nipples, tugging on the chain of the nipple clamps while sucking on my clit, just to drive me even wilder.

A success. A mind-blowing, epic success.

"Oh, my God."

My raised hands clutch at the pillows above me. Alistair hasn't permitted me to release them. I want more of this, I want to come. And for that to happen, I know I have to be good. Really, really good.

Swirling his tongue in one final circle around my pussy, Alistair lifts his head. He leaves the handle of the long clamp on my belly, and grabs my ass, hefting it in the air.

"Making sure it's nice and wet for the clamp."

He smirks a second before spitting on my hood. He smears it, using the smooth pad of his thumb, guaranteeing no part of my pussy is left dry. A pleasure so profound coats me in a blanket of lust, followed by an acute pain that has me screaming in surprise.

The clamp is fastened to my clit.

"Breathe, Nola."

Alistair doesn't remove it. He begins the task of undressing himself, button by button.

"I—I—"

"Do you remember the day I shoved my cock in your virgin little ass?"

His shirt is on the floor, his chest on display. My eyes feel like they're about to pop out of their sockets. I hold my breath, unable to do as he says. It's as if my mind convinces itself that if I do, I'll be subjected to a worse torment, one I can't and won't be able to handle.

"It hurt, at first." Alistair's cock is freed from his pants, erect and proud.

My agony doesn't frighten him. It's his to control, his to own.

I hold onto his words and those he said before. Nothing he does will cause irreparable damage.

I try clinging onto that promise, but it's so goddamn hard.

"Then it was better, wasn't it?"

He's on the bed, his lips in the place where the clamps connect to my pussy. Alistair slips his tongue out, lapping it on the outside of the clamp, stroking my squeezed clit. It's amorous. It's making me melt.

I breathe.

And I like it. I like this type of pain too.

"Yes, baby." With a final open kiss on my pussy, he stands up. "I knew reminding you my cock in your ass would do it for you."

He flips me on my stomach. The pressure on my nipples and clit intensifies due to gravity. I breathe once more, settling into the pain. Learning to love it.

Alistair, who's attuned to my body signals as though they were his, must see me taking it. He rubs my left ass cheek, opening me up for the lube he squirts over my pucker.

It warms at his touch; the rim first, the inside later. Two of Alistair's fingers stretch my sensitive tissues, opening me up to him. He takes them out, bends over me to grip my hair at the base of my skull, guiding the crown of his cock to my wanting asshole.

Alistair nudges it inside until it slides in.

We both grunt, our pleasured breaths mingling.

"Good thing I'm equally eager to fuck you there."

His words tickle the skin of my cheek.

Crude yet soft.

Allowing me a second of reprieve before he slams his shaft deep inside me.

CHAPTER TWELVE
Alistair

I've never been addicted to anything, not even my career.

Alcohol, drugs, gambling, even running, or any kind of physical activity… Plenty of my work partners or connections fell into one of those rabbit holes.

Not me.

I'm in control.

I *am* control.

The old me was, anyway.

This new person who loves Nola more than life itself, he holds a measure of control. It's only a part of him.

The other part is Nola.

I'm addicted, crazy, and madly possessed by this woman lying beneath me.

"Alistair," she rasps.

My fingers tangle in her hair. Each shove of my cock in her ass is matched with a tug of those long, wavy locks. Her cheek is plastered to the clean, white linens of the hotel, her lips open, eyes those of a wild animal.

Of a lioness.

And the queen of the animal kingdom can take just about anything.

"Your fucking ass, Nola." I bite her bare shoulder, sucking on the flesh.

Nola cries from her throat and eyes alike, yet she pushes her butt to match my thrusts.

My goddamn goddess.

"Who are these tears for, sweetheart?"

I release her hair, slipping my hand to the chain connecting her nipple clamps.

"For you."

"These tits?" I slow my thrusts, twisting the chain around my finger and pulling it to the right.

"You."

Without a foreword, I tug them to the left.

"You, what?"

"You, Daddy."

The fireworks planned for New Year's Eve tomorrow will have nothing on the bright light her total submission shines on me. My once-cold heart melts every day more for Nola. My damaged soul is repaired increment by increment thanks to her.

She doesn't just run her own company. She runs me.

Her cheeks are flushed, a sheen layer of sweat forms on her forehead. I bend to kiss and lick it off Nola, who shivers beneath me.

"Daddy makes you feel good?"

Leaving the chain, I trail my hand down her belly to the clit camp.

"Very."

"Are you ready to come?"

"Yes." The word erupts in a breathy sigh.

I flick the handle of the clamp. It dangles back and forth on my palm, swinging like a pendulum. I match the rolls of my hips to its beat, the whole unit of *us* swaying in tandem.

She stills briefly, her lips parting wider, her intake of breath shorter. She's about to come.

With my fingers curled around the handle of the clit clamp, I growl, "Do it."

The way her ass clenches on my cock nearly sends me over the edge, myself. But only after I give her what she needs.

I release the hold of the toy on her clit as the orgasm rips through her, her eyes closing on a throaty moan. She breaks into shivers, the fresh flow of blood to the area heightening her arousal.

It evolves and grows inside her. Having her scream my name with more urgency than ever before gives her away.

And I am not fucking done.

The dangling chain is my next target. Before Nola's tremors reach their end, I make sure she has an encore. Both the clamps rip off her nipples at once, and she shakes so badly I have to get rid of them to envelop her body with my arms and pull her back to my chest.

"Your ass is milking me, Nola." I rise, pounding her harder, faster. Squeezing either side of her waist, I tell her, "Gonna finish inside you, baby. Gonna give you my cum for being my good, obedient girl."

Murmurs of *yes* and *please* and *God* surround me in the symphony of our bodies slapping together. My orgasm starts at my lungs, whooshing to my stomach, coiling at my balls.

I let go, shoot my load, and keep thrusting until I'm spent. I come so hard, my orgasm drips from her even before I pull out. I take my cock out, spreading myself around her rim, massaging her buttocks.

It's selfish of me to marvel at her while she needs my care. But the relaxed smile on her face allows me another single moment in time to admire my woman, the wonder of her.

"My baby."

I kiss the small of her back, then pick her up to take her to the bathroom. Carefully, I lay her down on the pillows of the long bench they have there, running the hot water in the bath.

"You please me." My forehead presses to hers, my hand stroking her damp cheek. "Every day, sweetheart. Every minute. You always please me."

There's so much more to it. However, this isn't the moment for her to hear it, to truly understand the complexity of my emotions, to answer what I'm keen to ask her today instead of tomorrow.

It isn't, since this right here, it isn't about me. It's about the woman who offered me her body and soul to bend to my will. I'm indebted to her, for the gracious gift she grants me daily.

Tomorrow will be the day for declarations.

Tonight, the best I can and will do for her is let her process it with my silent care and affection.

"Thank you." Her palm grazes my stubbled cheek. "I love you."

"I love you, too." I cover her hand, drawing it to my lips and kissing each of her knuckles. "Would you like me to tie your hair up?"

I did it the first time she showered at my place. I didn't know what the love of a woman was back then, not to have it tear my insides, nor to have it doted on me. I knew what aftercare was, yet somehow, with Nola, it wasn't the same as the others before her. It was personal. It was something I wanted to last, even back then.

When I pinned her hair to keep it dry in the bath I ran for her, I felt like it was *right*. My gut sent me the memo long before my head could piece it together.

I've been a stubborn bastard for the longest time. And I intend to rectify it for the rest of my life.

"Yes, please." Her lips curl up by some.

I go to the bath, check the water temperature. It's hot. A little too hot. I close the tap, heading for my second mission.

The hair pins and the ribbon are in Nola's toiletry bag. I carry them to where she's reclined, placing them on a washcloth on the floor. Both my hands slip beneath her back and legs.

"Hold on to me," I say, and she does.

In measured movements, we descend to the floor. My feet press together, my legs resting in a diamond shape. My back leans on the bench, while Nola's is bare to me, other than her mane cascading down it.

Silently, I loop her hair around my fist. I smile to myself at the stark contrast of the intention behind the movement not ten minutes ago, to the end it serves now.

Nola angles her chin up, helping me to twist it up her head.

"Alistair?" she says, facing the wall ahead of her.

The second pin is in my hand, prepared to lodge into the bun I hold in place.

"Yes, sweetheart?"

"Do you…" Her voice is choked.

"Do I what?"

I'm eager to hear the question, to figure out what bothers her and wipe it off the face of the earth. Yet the constant reminder of her fragility in her current state levels my tone leads me to keep doing her hair peacefully.

She sighs, her shoulders slumping. From the side, I see the long lashes fluttering on her cheeks.

"Do you ever regret being with me?"

Fuck patience. I let go of the ribbon, spin Nola to her side and bend my knees to keep her extra warm on top of the room's heating system.

"Why would you say that?" I kiss her jaw, her cheek, massaging her back.

My pulse races, my head analyzing our interactions over the past two weeks. "If I've done something to offend you, to make you think you're anything less important to me than the air I breathe, tell me."

"It's not you." Her hands drape around my shoulders, nuzzling her nose to my neck.

I cup the back of her head, brushing my lips on the top of it. "Then what, my love?"

"Sometimes, times like today..." she trails off.

"Yes?"

"I know we started in this *teaching* sort of relationship." She rears her head back by some, gazing at me from below. "And I love it. I love us. I wouldn't change a thing. It's just that today I realized how unworldly I am. That I'm not enough for you."

The speech I have lined up for tomorrow nearly spills out of me. It'll clear things up for her in a heartbeat.

And it'll overwhelm her, might not even get through in the slumber her body slowly sinks into.

Without the option to spank these irrational thoughts out of her, I choose the other easy path, for now.

"This." I take her palm, pinning it to my chest. "It beats for you."

"Alistair."

"Quiet." Slithering our joined hands down my chest, I expand my lungs. "These, they breathe for you."

Her face scrunches, her eyes tearing up. I kiss her eyelids, then place her to the side so I can stand up and take her to the bath.

A crippling sense of incompetency accompanies me as I do, prevailing in every cell of my body. To have her cry in the aftermath of our sex in distress, it's my fucking fault. I should've insisted we sleep and play all she wants in the morning. Should've made her tea, placed her in the enveloping cocoon of the water immediately.

I remind myself this isn't about me. It's a lesson for the future, a mistake I won't regret. At the present moment, there's nothing to do other than continue putting effort into pacifying her.

I sit first, like Nola likes it, guiding her into the hot water to climb into my lap.

She relaxes into me, her tears at bay. I can finally breathe a little.

"Nola." Angling her cheek to my shoulder, I let my lips brush on her temple. "Trust me when I say this, I'm the one at a huge disadvantage here. Not you."

"Oh, please."

"Honest to God." I work out the short version of tomorrow's speech in my head. "I'm damaged. My trauma will haunt me for the rest of my life, and there's a good chance I might never rid myself of my guilt. You see through it, and you love me still. You stay."

"I love you," she whispers against my skin. "I love Jolene. I even love Connie."

The fact she mentions my deceased sister as well as Jolene, the only remaining member of my nuclear family, makes my heart lurch in my chest.

Makes me love her even more.

"I love you and your parents, too." I snuggle her closer to me. "And that's all that matters."

"Really?" She finds my gaze, light flecks of happiness dancing in her brown eyes.

"Yes." I kiss her nose. "And fuck me if I know how I got to be this lucky to have a woman who's such a pure essence of love and light. I don't and will never need or even think about anyone else."

She rolls her eyes. "You're so full of it."

"Enough of this." Her amusement consoles me enough to end our conversation for today. "Come on, now. Sit up and let me soap you up before the water runs cold."

She listens, allowing me to take care of her from lathering her body in soap, rinsing her clean until we end up in bed where we both fall asleep in each other's arms.

CHAPTER THIRTEEN
Nora

"Alistair?"

He's been uncharacteristically quiet. For the past five minutes or so, the man who usually bombards me with compliments, tucks a lock of hair behind my ear, or adjusts my dress to his liking has kept to his side of the room and hasn't said a word.

He blinks once. That's it.

His broad frame in a black tux remains perched on the dresser of the hotel suite, his hands firmly in his pockets.

And though I could've looked at him forever, at the slick, brushed-back hair and the stubble he groomed an hour ago, his silence unnerves me.

Just a little.

"Alistair?"

His lips tug to the side. "How may I be of assistance, ma'am?"

I'm momentarily stumped by the dangerous concoction in his eyes that bore into my soul and his Southern accent.

He doesn't use it much, not when he can help it. Brings up too many memories, he says. Deepens the longings for his family members who wait for him on the other side.

But when it does slip, when he's giving me another layer of his true self, I can't help that I'm befuddled. Glaring. Enamored up to my ears.

His.

"Nola?" It's his turn to rouse me out of my daydreams slash drooling. "You were saying?"

"You were staring," I blurt out, somewhat embarrassed I've been caught ogling.

"Excuse me?" His chuckle paints the room in streaks of elegant gold.

"You were staring at me."

His grin widens. "You're a beautiful woman, Nola."

"As if this is the first time you're seeing this dress. Which you bought." I regain my bearings. Partially. Enough to make sense of my thoughts. "And you were silent."

"Is that so?"

"Pensive."

The weight of his glare dips into my belly. I gulp.

He pushes off the dresser, crossing the short space to me. The room is almost entirely dark. Except for the light filtering out of the bathroom where I pinned my hair in a ponytail and applied my makeup minutes ago and the one lamp we left on, there's no other light.

A fact that highlights the darkening of Alistair's eyes. They turn shark-like black, perusing me, threatening to eat me whole.

"Can't a man appreciate his"—he backtracks on his words, rubbing his chin between his fingers. Then he starts over—"girlfriend?"

"He can," I pipe out.

He crowds my space, stealing my breath.

"Appreciate your elegant arms beneath these sheer sleeves?" His knuckles graze me, shoulder to wrist.

"Yes." Breathing is a luxury I'm losing fast.

Alistair spins to stand at my front, his hands at my waist. "Admire your curves in this tight, silk dress?"

"M-hmm."

Slipping one hand behind my back, he thrusts me into his taut chest and erection.

"To imagine what I'll have to do to arouse this fine woman."

I gasp, his unforgiving squeeze of my nipples sending me into purgatory. I'm burning in hell only to be shipped to the gates of heaven a second later.

"How much effort I'll have to put into stimulating those nipples once we're out." He flattens his palm on my collarbone, arching me back, pushing me lower. His lips hover over my nipple, his dark eyes glinting at me. "To have them poke through that dress, make you my little forbidden fruit for a short while."

His name permeates the suite as his teeth close on my nipple.

"I believe that's the look you were talking about," he growls.

Alistair shoves us to the wall, yanking my dress up to bunch around my thighs. He kicks my legs to either side, thrusting three fingers into my pussy.

"No panties." In harsh movements, he strokes the inside of my walls, shoving them to the knuckles. "My good little girl, doing what I told her to."

His teeth mark my bare neck, a hairbreadth from puncturing the skin. I cry out, gripping the side of his throat, the hair he so masterfully styled earlier.

Living with him is a constant match of push and pull. I want him close on one hand, needing him to stop biting me on the other.

But wanting him close always wins.

He leaves my pussy empty for the short length of time it takes him to whip out his cock. "I was going to wait, meant to have you at the top of the Eiffel, watching the fireworks while I fucked you until you couldn't breathe."

He grips my thigh, hitting a million nerve endings in his brutality. "But you had to open your mouth." Quicker than lightning, he grips my bottom lip in his teeth, as if to emphasize his point. "Had to be so goddamn tempting. You leave me no choice, Nola."

His wide tip spreads my folds, teasing me to no end.

"Gonna have to mess up your dress before we leave."

I grunt at the ruthless plunge of his dick into me. My back hits the wall, a sound that doesn't deter Alistair's forceful pummeling into me.

If anything, it's the other way around. He swells in my cunt, his free hand yanking at my hair. "Look at me."

"Yes, Daddy." My eyes open to gaze at his looming face.

"You've satisfied me greatly this trip." The rhythm of his pounding is harsh, his words coming out in grunts. "Really satisfied me."

Elation spreads on top of my skin, inside my veins. The praise and acknowledgment nudge at my orgasm faster than any toy would've.

"And good girls get their reward. They get a choice." His fist pulls my hair tighter when he sees my eyes starting to roll with pleasure. "Would you rather come while I fuck you or while you're riding my face?"

My core is wound tight, about to snap at his dirty talk.

He notices, growling, "Don't you come."

"With you fucking me," I scream my answer, the first thing my dazed mind offers me.

He says nothing else, pulls me off the wall, grabs a pink peony from the closest vase, and tumbles the both of us to the floor. Alistair adjusts my feet to loop around his neck, the flower he clutches between his teeth makes him look like the evil version of Zorro.

I fucking love it.

"Your pretty, pink clit went through a lot yesterday."

He rocks into me, slower but nowhere near tender. His hand slithers to my neck, his favorite place other than my pussy and heart. His fingers don't wrap around it, they're just there.

A distraction. For what he was doing with the peony while I closed my eyes, anticipating the pleasure of his grip.

The gentle tickle of my nub compared to the harsh fucking and the almost choking whooshes the air out of my lungs.

He spins it in circles, the same direction he sways his length inside of me.

"Will have to be kind to your sweet mound," he says through gritted teeth. "The rest of you, not so much."

The tightening of his hand on my throat happens the same moment his slow sways transform into rough thrusts one after the other. He pats, caresses, and pushes the petals of the peony on my clit.

It begins to tickle the edge of unbearable. I open my mouth to say something.

Alistair presses against my vocal cords. He never takes me to where I can't breathe, but he does demonstrate his absolute and total control. How safe I am under his watch.

"Don't run from it." His thumb strokes where my pulse hammers. "Let me take care of you. Let me make you come."

"Alistair."

"Come," he thunders.

His hair is mussed, his shirt scrunched, and he is still without a doubt, the most elegant, pristine king of my universe.

Smothered beneath him, subjected to his every desire, I come. The world shatters into a million tiny pieces around me, my body a vessel of roaring, pummeling pleasure.

Alistair releases my throat, just as fast as he released the clasps, prolonging my orgasm. As I gasp hard for air, Alistair's lips curve, seething, and in a few, demanding thrusts, his climax fills me.

I'm whole.

"I love you, Nola."

He caresses my chest, my neck, my chin, and my lips with the peony. It's soothing and enveloping. It also smells of my pussy and his sweat. Of us.

"I love you, too." I smile, tugging on his neck using my feet.

It amuses him. Following my subtle hint, he discards the flower, lowers my feet to the floor, and bends down to me.

One tender kiss is all he allows me before helping me up to prepare yet again for dinner.

CHAPTER FOURTEEN AND LAST
Nola

Alistair's hands wrap me like a warm blanket, his eyes delve deep into my heart, finding their home inside it.

It's ten minutes to midnight, in the restaurant Alistair closed for the night for us. The soft white lights they had on while we ate a delicious three-course meal are muted now, their hue a magical shade of amber.

We're swaying to *Baby* by Warpaint, a slow song that stands at complete odds with the celebrations going on beneath us. We have Paris at our feet. There's nothing to conceal the outside world from us. We're surrounded by walls of glass in every direction, front-row seats to the city I'll forever remember fondly in my heart.

It's beautiful. It's wonderful. It's undoubtedly one of the most epic sights I've ever witnessed, or ever will.

However—and I might be biased, though I don't give a fuck—having Alistair with me beats all of it. All the wonders of the world couldn't compare to the other half of me holding me tight.

"How did you like the meal?"

His hand travels the curve of my spine, slow and steady.

A prickling sensation ripples across my skin. "I liked it a lot."

"I'm happy." In an ever-tender gesture, Alistair presses his lips to my forehead. "I want you to enjoy life."

He gulps, pinning me with a meaningful gaze. "Always."

My love's slight pause reminds me of the pensiveness he brushed off back in the room.

I don't have much time to linger on it or ask him again.

The last note of the song plays. Silence ensues.

"Sweetheart," Alistair's call draws my focus back to him and nothing else.

I'm still glued to his mesmerizing eyes, though they're not above me anymore.

They're below me.

Alistair bends on one knee, popping open a square box.

With a diamond ring in it.

"Nola."

During my twenty-one years on this planet, I have considered plenty of things.

I wished to study economics in Seattle, and I went for it. I wanted to save enough money to start my own business—and I did whatever it took to get there. Having my own version of Toy Shop was a dream that became possible with the charity offering grants, so I applied there.

Many, many life-altering decisions.

None of which revolved around the concept of marriage.

None, until King Charming—despite the proper definition, Alistair cannot be called anything other than a king—demolished his way into my heart.

I should wait for him to continue, but my quivering mouth has other plans for me, "Oh my God. Oh my God. Oh my God."

Alistair takes one of my hands, kissing the back of it. A slow smirk plays on his handsome face. "That usually comes after."

"Shut up." I swipe a tear off my cheek, realizing I didn't mean what I said at all. "No, sorry. Don't shut up. Speak."

He nods, sobering quickly. He has on his impenetrable mask of brutal force, full of intention, not to be deterred.

"Nola Vickers. The first time you called me from Toy Shop, I knew there was something about you. More than your beautiful voice, more than your kindness to help a total stranger while obviously risking your job. Something about you just resonated with me on a deeper level, and I knew I had to have you. I wanted you, and yet I couldn't believe you agreed to meet me, but I did believe I was extremely fortunate that you had."

"You made a pretty convincing argument," I say past the tears.

"Sweetheart." He kisses the inside of my wrist. "How I love your tender heart."

"Thank you."

"In fact, I love all of you." Alistair lets out a huff of a laugh. "I love the scent you leave in the bedroom we share, your snarky retorts, your ability to trust and give yourself to me time and time again. I don't take it for granted. I don't take your smiles for granted, or the constant sunshine you grace my life with."

His eyebrows knead together. "What you said yesterday, about not being worthy. Baby, I'm blessed beyond any reasonable doubt to have you as my partner. To have you choose me outdoes any physical possession I own, any cent I earned. I was a poor man before you came along, and I'll be a poor man if you leave."

"I won't."

Joy illuminates his rugged face.

"This belonged to my mother." He removes it from the box, holding it on the ring finger on my left hand.

So, this is what a heart attack feels like. I hope not to die before I can at least say yes.

"Will you do me the honor of being its new owner? Of being my wife?"

"Alistair." I slap a shaky palm to my lips. "What about Jolene?"

"She practically begged me to pass it over to you. To us." He clears his throat. "Your father gave us his blessing, too."

"Dad?"

"Yes. I asked him a week ago."

"Alistair," I repeat his name. It's so hard to say anything else.

"Is that a yes?"

"Yes! Yes!" I wait for the whole second it takes him to slip the polished Asscher-cut ring on my finger.

After that, I leap on him. We fall to the concrete floor, hugging, smiling, kissing.

"I love you so much," I mumble against his lips.

"So do I, sweetheart." He hugs me as if his life depends on it. "So do I."

It's going to be a great year.

About the Author
Writing edgy spicy novellas, addicted to HEAs, and an avid plant lady.

Stay in Touch!
Newsletter for new releases: https://bit.ly/3c3K2nt
Instagram: https://bit.ly/3QQ3Nh4
TikTok: https://www.tiktok.com/@evamarkswrites
Facebook Group: https://bit.ly/3LnFpln
Website: https://www.evamarkswrites.com

Toy Shop, Adult Games Book 1

Time to strap on, because class is about to start…

Working in an adult toy shop doesn't make me an expert on the matter. Quite the opposite, actually. My experience with my last boyfriend all but destroyed my interest in it.

Until billionaire Alistair Cromwell bulldozed his way into my life.

He's unlike anyone I've ever known—dominant, harsh, but oddly tender. And he's more than willing to educate me on every product in the shop.

In fact, he *insists* on it.

He tells me I'm his good girl. That only I can save him from his demons. I want that desperately. But I also want the one thing he doesn't think he can ever give me.

His heart.

Well, he's about to learn that while I'm not worldly when it comes to toys, I do know a thing or two about love.

And I'm going to teach him every bit as much as he's taught me…

TW: Bondage, BDSM, edge play, breath play, sex toys, a bit of degradation.

Available on Amazon

Have you read the Blue series?

Little Blue, Book 1

I worked for Hudson Kent for years.
He's not a man you refuse.
But I did.
Because no matter how much I wanted him, chasing the sexy, older CFO would've ruined the reputation I worked so hard to build. It just wasn't a risk I was willing to take.
Until now.
Hudson isn't my boss anymore. There's nothing stopping us from acting on our mutual attraction and acting out every dirty fantasy we've ever had.
So, if he calls me now, there's only one reply I can give.
Yes, Sir..

TW: Bondage, BDSM, a bit of degradation.

Available on Amazon

Have you read the Blue series?

Little Halloween, Book 2

This holiday he plans on a special trick and treat for her…

After overcoming our differences, I'm finally engaged to Hudson, my old boss and millionaire CFO.

We're madly in love and I can't complain when he constantly cherishes, coddles me and says I'm his good girl. I can't and won't, even if I miss his harsh domineering side at times.

But my fiancé, who reads me like a book, can tell I have doubts, and he knows just how to put them to rest.

This Halloween, at an adult club party, Hudson will show me and everyone around once and for all exactly what my Sir is made of.

TW: Bondage, BDSM, pet play, sex club, exhibitionism, a bit of degradation and a whole lot of love.

Available on Amazon

Coming February, 2023

Little Valentine, Book 3 in the Blue series

Running a business with Hudson who's my husband, soulmate and Dominant can be as rewarding as it is challenging.

I want to keep pleasing him, be his good girl and the hardworking woman he married and fell in love with.

But when I'm so tired, distracted by my sense of smell that works overtime and uncomfortably bloated, it's hard.

Maybe that's why when Hudson sees through me and demands I take some time off after our Valentine's day tonight, I say yes in a heartbeat.

Because, really, that's all I need. Some rest.

Right?

TW: Bondage, BDSM, pet play, a bit of degradation and a whole lot of love.

Pre-order on Amazon

Printed in Great Britain
by Amazon